A church is a weighty thing, isn't it? Its doors are heavy and hard to budge. Its walls are made of stone. The steps you climb to enter it can make your legs tired. If the ceiling is very high, you might feel very small.

And a church might have pictures of people or things that are scary.

Still, there are many good reasons to visit a church.

One reason is to look at the pictures to find out what the people who made them believed. And the pictures almost always tell stories.

My mother had a special way to visit a church—it was light, not scary, and even kind of floaty.

We called it

SAINT SPOTTING

SAINT SPOTTING

OR

HOW TO READ A CHURCH

CHRIS RASCHKA

EERDMANS BOOKS FOR YOUNG READERS

GRAND RAPIDS, MICHIGAN

Published in 2021 by
Eerdmans Books for Young Readers
an imprint of Wm. B. Eerdmans Publishing Co.
Grand Rapids, Michigan • www.eerdmans.com/youngreaders

29 28 27 26 25 24 23 22 21   1 2 3 4 5 6 7 8 9

A catalog record of this book is available
from the Library of Congress.

ISBN 978-0-8028-5521-3

Illustrations created with
watercolor.

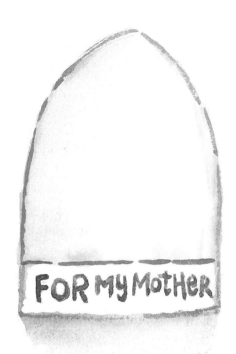

FOR My MOTHER

H ere's how you do it.

Look at this map. It shows you all
the saints we'll spot today.

1 St. ANTHONY
2 St. RITA
3 St. CATHERINE
4 St. AGNES
5 St. ANDREW
6 St. SEBASTIAN
7 St. BARTHOLOMEW
8 St. ZENO
9 St. FRANCIS
10 St. LUCY
11 St. CECILIA
12 St. NICHOLAS
13 St. PETER
14 St. PAUL
15 St. MATTHEW
16 St. MARK
17 St. LUKE
18 St. JOHN
19 St. MARY AND JESUS
20 St. ELIZABETH
21 St. MARY MAGDALENE
22 St. JOHN THE BAPTIST
23 JESUS CHRIST
24 St. JOSEPH
25 St. MARTHA
26 St. CHRISTOPHER
27 St. BARBARA
28 FAITH
29 HOPE
30 CHARITY
31 St. BRIDGET
32 St. JEROME
33 St. AUGUSTINE
34 St. EUSTACE
35 St. MONICA
36 St. ROSE OF LIMA
37 St. MARGARET
38 St. GEORGE

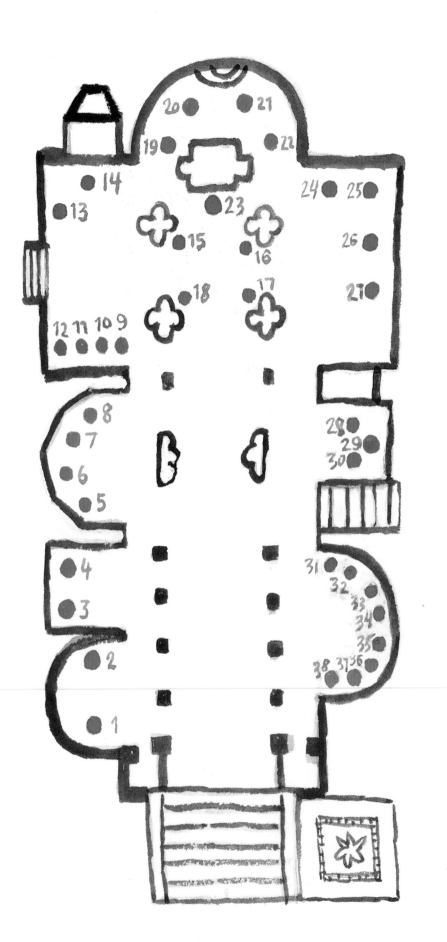

SAINT ANTHONY

S aints are people who are important in the history of the Christian faith.

SAINT RITA

They always have stories of their own which give you clues to recognize them.

For instance, Saint Anthony was kind and loved reading, so you will see him holding a book or a baby (usually Jesus as a baby) or both.

And Saint Rita had a wound which never healed. She is the saint of suffering. Sometimes people think of her when something has been bothering them for a long time too.

When saints are killed for what they believe, they are called martyrs.

Here is Saint Catherine with her wheel, which was made to kill her as punishment for teaching the emperor's wife about Jesus. When the wheel failed, poor Saint Catherine was killed with a sword.

The symbol for Saint Agnes is a lamb.

Both of these saints were killed because they refused to marry the rich men who desired them. They wanted to live simply, as nuns.

Nuns study, serve, and pray.

St. ANDREW   St. SEBASTIAN

Sometimes a saint's symbol has something to do with how they were martyred, but not always.

St. BARtHOLOMEW

SAiNt ZENO

Here are four saints and their symbols:
Saint Andrew—an X-shaped cross.
Saint Sebastian—arrows.
Saint Bartholomew—his own skin.
Saint Zeno—a fishing pole.

Saint Zeno might or might not have
been martyred (it's a complicated
story) but he certainly wasn't
martyred with a fishing pole.
He just liked to fish!

Saint Sebastian was always my favorite
because he's easy to spot.

More saints and symbols:

Saint Nicholas's symbol is three bags of gold, which he gave to the poor. Our story of Santa Claus comes from him.

Saint Cecilia–musical instruments.

Saint Lucy–her eyes. She is the saint of vision. (Pictures of Saint Lucy always terrified me.)

Saint Francis is the saint of animals. He preached to the birds and called them his little brothers and sisters, which made people think he was crazy (but which is true if you think about it the way Saint Francis did).

SAINT NICHOLAS

SAINT CECILIA

SAINT LUCY

SAINT FRANCIS

Saint Peter carries
a key, which is the key
to heaven that Jesus gave him.
It could also mean knowledge and
understanding.

Saint Paul carries a book to show us
his great wisdom and learning. He
also might have a sword, not because
he was a soldier but because that
was how he was killed.

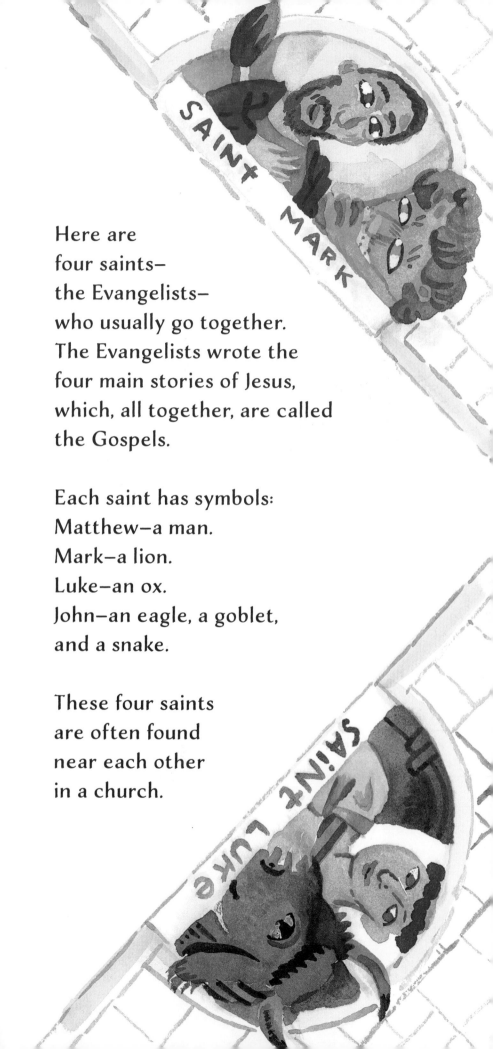

Here are
four saints—
the Evangelists—
who usually go together.
The Evangelists wrote the
four main stories of Jesus,
which, all together, are called
the Gospels.

Each saint has symbols:
Matthew—a man.
Mark—a lion.
Luke—an ox.
John—an eagle, a goblet,
and a snake.

These four saints
are often found
near each other
in a church.

SAINT MARY AND JESUS

Now we're coming to the front
of the church.

Here is Saint Mary,
the mother of Jesus.
She is also called
the Holy Mother,
the Madonna, or the
Blessed Virgin Mary.
You usually see her
holding the baby Jesus
in her lap, so she's
easy to find.

SAiNt ELiZaBEtH

Saint Elizabeth was Mary's cousin and the mother of Saint John the Baptist. Saint Elizabeth thought she was too old to have a baby (she was much older than Mary) but John was born in spite of her doubts.

SAINT MARY MAGDALENE

Saint Mary
Magdalene was a
friend and follower of
Jesus. Her symbols are long
hair and a jar of ointment.

Saint John the Baptist told
everyone that Jesus was coming.
Saint John the Baptist's symbols
are a long-stemmed cross, a fur
cloak, a honey pot or hive
(because he lived in
the wilderness), and
a lamb (which itself
represents Jesus).

SAiNt JOHN THE BAPTiST

Jesus is the reason for
churches being around at all.
People who believe in the stories
and teachings of Jesus are called
Christians, and churches are
their holy places.

And here at last is Jesus.
Jesus is also called Jesus
Christ. Christ is a Greek word
meaning Messiah, or chosen one.
Jesus is always found at the most
holy spot in a church: above or
behind the altar.

Jesus +++ Christ

Christians believe Jesus was a
living person, like all people, but
also divine, because he is the Son
of God. Jesus is often shown on a
cross, just before his death. This
is meant to emphasize his real life
and death. When he looks down,
we know that he cares for all in
life who suffer. His symbols are a
cross, a fish, or a lamb.

SAINT JOSEPH

SAINT MARTHA

Saint Joseph was the earthly
father of Jesus. He is remembered
for poverty, chastity, and
obedience. His symbols are
carpenter's tools.

Saint Martha was another friend
of Jesus. Her symbol is a ladle,
because she loved to serve.

SAINt CHRIStoPHeR

Sometimes a church may give you
stories, like these two, that are
not found in the Bible.

In his legend, Saint Christopher
carried the baby Jesus across a
river, and Jesus grew into a man
as they went.

Saint Christopher's symbols are
the baby Jesus and a staff.

SAINt BARBARA

Saint Barbara was shut into a tower by her father. Alone, she studied the sky and the stars and came to believe in the teachings of Jesus.

Her symbol is a tower.

These aren't saints really but ideas.

Faith—a cross.
Hope—an anchor.
Charity—a heart.

If you find yourself in a church with no saints, then you are probably in a Protestant church. Five hundred years ago, Protestant Christians protested against some of the doings of the Roman Catholic Church, which was the main church of Christians in the western world at that time. Among their protests was this: There are too many saints!

So that's how my mother and I visit
a church. She likes the paintings
and stories. I like the arrows.

Once, churches were called the Bibles
of the Poor. Even if you didn't have a
Bible (and no one besides priests and
monks and nuns did back then), and
even if you couldn't read, you could

learn all the important stories by
studying the pictures you saw on the
old churches' walls.

Saint Sebastian is still my favorite.